WARNING

This book contains adult language and violence. It may be considered offensive to some readers. This book is for sale to adults ONLY.

* * * * * * * * * * * * * * * * * *

Please store your files wisely where they cannot be accessed by underage readers.

ISBN-13: 978-1773500782
ISBN-10: 1773500783

Other Books by Freddie Kim:

<u>The Time Guardian Thriller Series</u>

When the Time Guardian goes missing, it is up to Sonia to travel back to the past the rectify the future of humanity. Follow this epic tale of good versus evil in the battle to control Earth's destiny.

<u>The Cyber Heist Files</u>

The entire financial industry of the World Government is at risk when a weaponized virus is covertly uploaded into the computer system. Faced with an imminent crisis, the government releases the whistle blower, Tyler Wilkens, in exchange for eradicating the virus that has infected their computer systems. Something malevolent is afoot and Wilkens is the best chance the government has to combat it.

Get the latest update on new releases from the author at:

https://www.freddiekim.com/newsletter/

This is a stand-alone story that is related to, but precedes, the events in "The Time Guardian Thriller Series"

Stinger Jacked

By Freddie Kim

Table of Contents

Chapter One

THE ASSAULT ship sat in the makeshift bay pending a software upgrade after an emergency landing for repairs. The cold, dry wind howled relentlessly, serving as a cloak for a pending clandestine operation.

Specialist Joseph Brunner remained crouched in the shadows. The rest of the members of the six-person tactical team were hidden, awaiting the order from their leader, Garon Rogal, to board the scantily guarded vessel.

Their mission, to steal an intact Stinger Class assault ship from the ka'Thar, was crazy, to say the least. Even crazier was breaking into an OmniClon Universal (OCU) outpost to do it. The resistance knew that the OCU had state-of-the-art equipment, making the task nearly impossible. Also, they had access to advanced technology supplied by their alliance partner, the ka'Thar. Essentially, the team had volunteered for a suicide mission.

In desperation, the Free Humanity Movement (FHM), the resistance force fighting for the liberation of humanity represented as the Versapiens, had hastily sent a small team to hijack the ship. No one had ever accomplished such a feat, and nothing this risky had even been attempted. The resistance had lost entire tactical teams to less daunting missions. But the grand prize made the cost in lives worth the risk.

Brunner was not supposed to be there. He had not planned his life that way. Although he volunteered to fight for the resistance, he never wanted to be a soldier. He thought he could contribute somehow in other ways. With a genius IQ, Brunner was more comfortable behind a desk, punching away on a keyboard, building computer models, programming, and analyzing data.

But today, the FHM did not need him behind a desk. Instead, they needed his on-the-fly expertise with uploading a virus into the target ship's system to allow the small tactical team the ability to access the core systems and steal the ship. Brunner's skills were needed for a critical role in the mission. The pressure he felt was beyond anything he had ever experienced.

Twenty-Four Hours Earlier

"Can we trust this intel?" asked Lieutenant Garon Rogal.

"It's good. I vouch for the source with my life," answered Herm Mellitz, the Intelligence Officer.

"We need you to put a team together, and do it fast," said Commander Statton. "You have a twenty-four-hour window before the ship joins the ranks of the OCU's regular fleet. There is no telling when we'll get such an opportunity again."

Rogal furrowed his brows. The intel was like a gift from heaven, and it would be a waste not to act on it. It wasn't every day a ka'Thar ship required emergency service from an OCU outpost. Especially from an easily accessible outpost with an established routine. He perceived many areas of concern. This could be their first and last opportunity to acquire an assault ship of their own. If they failed, their hand would be revealed, and the OCU would surely tighten up security measures to counter any future attempts.

"Under normal circumstances, it would take at least a month to plan and train for such a mission, and the outcome at best would be eighty percent successful," said Rogal. "But these aren't normal circumstances. We've been hit hard by the OCU, losing over fifty percent of our forces these past six months." His demeanor hardened, having warned Command against squandering resources needlessly in low-yield, high-casualty missions.

The jab was not lost on Statton. He had had to answer to his superiors for the dismal performance of those under him. Although a brilliant tactician, Rogal was a thorn in his side. Somehow Rogal remained insulated from the watchful eyes of Command as his missions continued to yield results. He was a rare breed, having led more than thirty successful missions so far. Most of his peers, the other mission leaders, didn't make it past ten missions, losing entire teams in the process.

Rogal's legendary stature had afforded him a few privileges which included second-guessing and criticizing some of his own commander's orders. Fortunately for him, the resistance did not mete out strict disciplinary action like their OCU counterpart did.

"Lieutenant, I am quite aware of how thin our resources are. Everyone has been asked to step up. The way I see it, we have no choice but to push ahead with this mission," said Statton, finding the hook he needed to get Rogal on board. "The resistance needs a win. Morale is at an all-time low. If we let this opportunity pass us by without at least attempting a mission, we might as well give up and hand ourselves over to the ka'Thar. I'm sure they'd be happy to take willing victims."

"The commander has a valid point. If this mission fails, no one would be the wiser, and morale will remain low. However, if the mission succeeds, it'll go a long way in justifying our methods and very existence," said Mellitz. "There's a bigger issue at hand, and few in the resistance are aware of it. Rogal, you've probably heard the rumors."

Rogal nodded, feeling the dread wash over him. So, the rumors were true. This changed the game, and they all knew it. "I suspected as much. Why am I hearing about this now for the first time? You know where I stand."

The ka'Thar supplied the assault ships to the OCU, who were now able to step up their campaign of terror among the poorly defended Versapien settlements. Prior to this revealing discussion, the official word was that these attacks on the settlements were isolated occurrences. But Rogal knew better. He had witnessed first-hand the destruction wrought by the opposition, especially with advanced weaponry. The Versapiens didn't stand a chance.

Command thought it wise to keep the increase in frequency of OCU attacks secret so as not to demoralize the spirits of the people they were fighting for. Hopelessness didn't make for a good campaign slogan. Rogal thought otherwise. If the people knew what was going on with the settlements, then the FHM would be able to convince more able bodies to join the resistance. As it was, the only recruits were those who had directly lost loved ones at the hand of the enemy. His experience taught him that individuals would generally step up when faced with adversity.

Chapter Two

Joseph Brunner was one of those recruits who joined the resistance after the OCU pillaged his village and collected his parents and everyone else for the ka'Thar Harvest. The enemy alliance treated the Versapiens like chattel, sending their captives to another part of the universe to supply the ka'Thar war machine in their efforts to conquer every race that posed a threat.

Although not much in the way of stature or bravery, Brunner grew incensed enough to join the resistance. Maybe he couldn't fight in the trenches, but he could contribute in other ways. His advanced intellect allowed him the versatility to excel at anything he put his mind to.

It surprised him when he was called to an emergency meeting with Lieutenant Rogal. The only contact he had ever had with mission leaders was when they needed clarification of information or use of software for critical missions. The young specialist knew Rogal was a results-driven leader who demanded loyalty and perfection from those under his command. Frankly, it scared Brunner.

<<◇>>

"I'll be honest with you. You aren't my first choice for this mission. In fact, you wouldn't even be my second choice," said Rogal to the five resistance fighters gathered in the briefing room. "You lack discipline, training, and experience. None of you have even worked together as a team."

"Then why are we here?" asked Sergeant Dalton. He barely hid his insolence as he asked the question. Except for Brunner, the others nodded in unison, awaiting Rogal's explanation.

"Believe it or not, you're the best I've got right now. Each of you has the skills to complete this mission with some degree of success. Hell, I'll take ten percent odds at this point," said Rogal, as he looked each team member in the eye, one by one. "Make no mistake. This is a dangerous mission, and some or all of us may not make it back."

"Ah, Lieutenant," said Brunner, raising his hand slightly. "I think you made a mistake. I'm a keyboard jockey, not a fighter."

The other four teammates chuckled at Brunner's display of timidity.

"Shut up, Brunner," yelled Rogal. He shot the specialist an angry glance. "Everyone in the resistance is a soldier. Everyone fights when called upon. When I assign you to my team, you fight. You fight for your team members, and you fight for the mission. You leave the thinking to me. Nothing else matters. Anyone have a problem with that?" He stared the other soldiers down.

"No, sir," they said.

"What? I can't hear you," shouted Rogal.

This time, all five members, including Brunner, shouted, "Sir. No, sir!"

Chapter Three

As Brunner waited in the shadows, he felt unduly encumbered by his heavy equipment. He'd brought as much as he could carry. Enough to cover up to ninety-nine percent of any contingencies he might encounter. Loaded with electronics and miscellaneous tools, he wished he had better intel. It could have cut the equipment down to twenty percent of what he carried now. He hoped nothing got damaged or else the mission would be a failure even before it really began.

His sidearm jabbed him in the ribs as it caught on the edge of a metal canister. His rifle blaster strap had slipped from his shoulder and dangled off the crook of his arm as he tried to adjust his backpack. His teammates carried sidearms and rifle blasters as well, but somehow they managed to wear their gear like extensions of their own bodies, which made him envious.

From his vantage point, Brunner could see all his teammates. Sergeant Harry Dalton was second in command for this mission and liked to talk a lot. Not that he had much to say. Most of what came out of his mouth was either an insult or a smart-ass comment. His early male-pattern baldness didn't diminish the sourness in his demeanor.

There was also Terese Landon. She doubled as the medic. Brunner suspected her combat skills were better than her bedside manners. If she wasn't literally dressed to kill in full combat gear, he could see himself being attracted to her.

The last two members, Miguel Hernandez and Ian Farkas, were relatively non-descript and uninteresting. Like generic soldiers, they possessed no special skill other than providing the muscle needed to complete the mission.

And then there was himself. A soldier wannabe who happened to be in the wrong place at a most inconvenient time. He was a loner and only felt comfort in solitude. He never had the urge to be part of a team, and being part of this particular team reinforced it.

Rogal gave the signal to advance. Sergeant Dalton was the first to go. The interval of time when that section of the ship was left unguarded allowed him to close the distance a few meters at a time. Dalton used the obstacles in his surroundings to evade detection.

Just before the OCU security guard showed up during his rounds, Dalton ran toward the metal boarding ramp of the ship and hid. When the guard appeared, Dalton snuck up behind him and butted the unsuspecting sentry on his head with the end of the rifle blaster.

The guard fell to the ground. Dalton dragged the body to the side and hid it under the ramp. The whole sequence was over in a matter of seconds. Dalton's movements were precise and executed without pause or hesitation. Brunner had no idea if the guard was dead, but he suddenly realized he was part of a team of efficient, trained killers. It was a good thing Dalton was on their side.

Rogal signaled for the remaining team members to approach. Brunner stood and ran as fast as he could under the circumstances, while still trying to adjust the heavy backpack on his shoulders, his rifle blaster swinging wildly off his arm.

The rest of the team had already reached the ship and waited for Brunner as he climbed the ramp. They snickered at his clumsiness while Rogal glared at him. Brunner was definitely out of his comfort zone. He was poorly prepared in the area of subterfuge and combat. How his teammates could carry so much weight in equipment with ease and without breaking a sweat, he had no idea.

"Your lack of organization and preparedness can make the difference between life and death for this team and the mission," Rogal reprimanded. "I suggest you get your act together."

Landon stepped up to Brunner and grabbed the straps of his backpack. "Here, let me help you with that," she said, as she yanked and tightened the loose straps. She gave him a wink and a smirk while the other three grunts tried to hide their amusement.

Just then it occurred to Brunner that one of them must have tampered with his backpack straps just before the mad dash to the ship. It was a stupid prank, and it made him look bad in front of his leader. He realized he was at the bottom of the pecking order and they had not yet accepted him as a full team member.

"Brunner, you're with me," said Rogal. "The rest of you, fan out and make sure the ship is secure. Complete your assignments and await further orders. Maintain radio silence for now."

For a fleeting moment, Brunner wondered what his teammates' assignments were, but his own pending assignment loomed ahead of him and the moment was gone. He was scared. Nothing had prepared him for this moment and he knew he was vulnerable. He didn't want to let the team down. He didn't want to fail. He certainly didn't want to die.

It was a small ship, so locating the bridge took no time at all.

Brunner shoved his fear aside and inspected the control console. He had never seen the architecture up close in real life, but he was familiar with the schematics, having poured over what little intel the resistance was able to accumulate over the years.

Still, navigating the alien technology would require creative thinking and finesse. It looked confusing at first, but once he figured out the basic logic, everything else fell into place. The technology was in his comfort zone. His fear stayed hidden in his gut.

"How long?" asked Rogal.

Brunner pressed a few icons and called up a series of displays on the console screen. "Hmmm. Strange. It looks like the original program was overlaid with a patch program. I'll have to make a few adjustments to compensate. My best guess for the time to upload the override program and complete the integration is twenty minutes. We've never done anything like this before except in simulations."

"Do you need to access the system core?"

Brunner glanced up and looked Rogal in the eyes. "No, everything can be done at this terminal, barring any unforeseen circumstances," he answered, hoping confidence oozed from his voice. This was his arena now, his specialty, his one chance at being the hero.

"Do it," said Rogal. He gave Brunner a nod of approval as if to convey his faith in the specialist's abilities.

"Yes, sir," said Brunner, as he discarded the rifle blaster and unpacked the heavy electronic equipment. After selecting a few items, he tossed the rest of the equipment aside and out of his way. He quickly connected the bypass controller and hard-wired a connection to his tablet.

The tablet lit up with a green icon labeled **<Ready for Upload—Press to Continue>**.

"Here we go." He pressed the icon, and the display changed to show a progress bar. "Now we wait." Brunner let out a sigh and took a seat behind the conn.

Rogal seemed to relax for a moment and looked at his watch. "The rest of the team should be set by —"

A shot rang out from somewhere within the ship. Brunner sat up and put his hand on his sidearm, his fingers shaking.

Rogal stiffened and looked toward the bridge entrance, a flash of worry on his face mixed with determination. He activated his communicator and broke radio silence. "Report!"

The communicator crackled, and Dalton's voice came on. "LT, we've been discovered. Holding our positions."

Brunner admired how Dalton and Rogal remained calm and kept their wits about them, despite the threatening situation. They didn't display the fear that haunted Brunner. He dared not show that he was scared. He didn't want to be a liability as the well-seasoned soldiers operated in military precision.

"On my way," answered Rogal. He turned to Brunner. "You stay here and make sure the program completes the upload. Hold this position and don't let anyone other than the team enter the bridge." He checked his sidearm and rifle blaster. "By holding this position, I mean use your rifle blaster if necessary. Keep the door locked after I leave."

Rogal left the bridge and scurried toward the disturbance in the ship. After Brunner activated the magnetic door lock, he grabbed his rifle blaster and crouched down under the control console, his weapon ready and aimed at the door. It was going to be a long twenty minutes.

Chapter Four

With the bridge sealed tight, no outside noise from the rest of the ship penetrated the soundproof walls.

Just before the twenty minutes had elapsed, a short, soft beep emitted from the console. That went off without a hitch. And just a minute to spare.

Brunner got up slowly from his crouched position beneath the console. His legs were stiff, and every part of his body ached from the awkward position. His heart skipped a beat as he read the screen on the console.

A message flashed across the screen in red block letters. **<Upload Progress Halted. Disable Virus Transmission Restrainer (VTR) to Complete Upload>**

This was something new. Brunner punched a few buttons to call up the system schematics on the console screen. Crap. The VTR was located at the system core. He would have to find it after all.

After searching the ship's database, Brunner found the engineering systems and called up the ship's schematics. He was in luck. The core was located close to the bridge. Unfortunately, Brunner wasn't able to access that particular part of the ship. The damned ka'Thar didn't make it easy. He unlocked the door to the bridge and tried to find access to the system core chamber from the other side.

Once he stepped into the corridor outside the bridge, Brunner heard shouting and blaster fire, making it hard to concentrate on finding the core's access panel. The hallway led away from the bridge in a circular path to the left and right directions, but not around it.

Brunner went down the left corridor and checked every panel he could find, but they were mostly access covers for circuit nodes or conduit joints. As he worked his way farther away from the bridge, the sound of running footsteps and shouting got nearer and louder.

"Everyone, retreat. Move toward the bridge!"

It was Commander Rogal with the rest of the team on his heels. Blaster fire erupted around them as they continued running toward Brunner's general direction, returning fire every few steps.

The bridge! Brunner had left his post. If they lost the position, it was game over, and his career with the resistance also would be over before it even really started. Without further hesitation, Brunner scrambled back toward the bridge.

"Dalton, Landon, hold this position and make sure they don't cross that corridor," commanded Rogal. "Hernandez, Farkas, cover the right side. No one passes."

With the team keeping the OCU forces at bay in the corridor, Rogal stepped onto the bridge. "How are we doing with the upload?"

Brunner didn't respond right away as he studied the ship's schematics. Quick, think. Where can the access panel be? He looked around the bridge and focused on where the system core chamber should be in relation to the bridge. Then he saw it. Or at least he imagined it. He stared at a section of the wall of the bridge, the only section that didn't have a workstation or any instrumentation over it.

It had to be there. If it wasn't, they would have to fight their way out somehow.

"Just another moment," answered Brunner as he strode right up to the wall. He ran his hands along the seams, but they were solid and unyielding. In a fit of desperation, or inspiration, he didn't really know, Brunner cast down his goggles over his eyes and switched to infrared. He scanned the wall slowly and saw a faint rectangular outline at the level of his waist a few centimeters away from a vertical wall seam.

He pressed the rectangular outline which gave way to the pressure. A hissing sound emitted from the seams as the air pressure equalized and the wall opened up like a door. Brunner surmised the chamber might have its own life support system.

By this time, OCU security had forced the four resistance fighters toward the bridge entrance from the corridor. Farkas was shot, but he was still breathing.

"Everyone, get in," yelled Rogal.

Farkas was dragged to safety by his gear straps. Once everyone was on the bridge, the last one, Dalton, closed the bridge door and activated the mag-lock. "That should buy us a few minutes before they either cut down or blow up the door."

"Brunner, anytime now. At your leisure." Rogal remained calm, but his voice carried an insistent undertone.

Chapter Five

Brunner was feeling the pressure. While the others covered the bridge door, he rushed blindly into the dark system core chamber. Along one side of the wall was an array of system cabinets. In his mad dash to find the VTR, he bumped into an overhead rafter beam that must have come loose from a previous military engagement. He fell back onto something pliant and giving. The sound of slight crunching accompanied his soft landing.

Without acknowledging the fall, Brunner quickly rose and rubbed his head. A bump had formed over the tender area. A small object dislodged from somewhere behind him and clinked on the corrugated floor.

The sound made Brunner pause. He looked down at his feet and saw a metallic beetle-shaped object. It had a lighted red slit down the middle and looked intriguing. He picked it up and stuffed it into his pocket. There would be plenty of time to examine it later, he hoped.

There was a more pressing issue at hand. He focused on the indicator lights of the instrument panels in the chamber to take his mind off the throbbing in his head. Embedded within the instrumentation was an input terminal. Brunner found the VTR switch and turned it off.

"Dalton, are all the charges in place?" asked Rogal.

"Yes, sir," answered the sergeant. "It's rigged to blow the plasma engines. The ship will be torn into a million pieces."

"What?" exclaimed Brunner as he watched Rogal pull out the remote detonator and activate it. "I didn't get the memo this was a suicide mission."

"Blowing up the ship is Plan B and not something you needed to know. Your only task is to get this ship flying. We can't let the enemy keep it. The FHM intends to destroy the OCU's growing fleet, and we'll do it one ship at a time if we have to," said Rogal.

"But we're still on it. Shouldn't we try to get away first?" said Brunner. His heart raced faster, and suddenly he was aware of the sweat dripping down his forehead.

"We all knew there was a good chance we wouldn't return," said Rogal. "If you can't get control of this ship before they cut open the door, this is our last resort. So, suck it up, soldier."

"It's too soon to call. The upload should be almost done," said Brunner.

He looked at the console screen which read < **Virus Transmission Restrainer (VTR) Disabled. Press to Continue Upload>**

He pressed the icon on the screen, and a progress bar appeared on the display. Brunner gasped in frustration. The display indicated that the upload would take another ten minutes. That was ten minutes they didn't have.

<<◇>>

The enemy was close to cutting away the door as the sparks and melted metal continued to light up their progress.

"Brunner, what do you need to do once the upload is completed?" asked Rogal.

"I just need to transfer full control of the ship to the remote tablet," answered Brunner. He showed Rogal the infographic.

Rogal placed a finger on the tablet, swiped through the information, and then nodded in comprehension.

"Everybody, switch out your batteries and make sure you have fresh ones in your rifles. Every second counts now," ordered Rogal. "We hold this bridge until we can't. Then we blow the whole damn thing to kingdom come. Dalton, Landon. Move Farkas into the core chamber when you're ready."

Hernandez struggled with his rifle, frustrated. "Damn, the battery release is stuck." He banged it against one of the instrument panels but to no avail.

Brunner searched his pockets for a suitable tool and found the oddly shaped beetle object he had picked up earlier. He took it out and studied it. The metal appendages sticking out from it were perfect for jogging the release mechanism loose. In his excitement, Brunner's voice rose as he squeaked, "Here, use this." He tossed the beetle tool to Hernandez.

With one hand, Hernandez caught the makeshift tool and quickly repaired his rifle. Then he tossed it back to Brunner and gave him an eager thumbs-up.

Brunner was distracted trying to get the viral program to finish uploading and didn't notice the toss. The metal beetle-like object bounced off the instrument panel in front of him and landed by Rogal's foot.

The red light on the object caught Rogal's eye. As he bent down to pick it up, he asked, "Where did you get this?"

Brunner cocked his head toward the system core chamber. "In there. I found it in there. Not sure what it is, though."

Rogal walked over to the core chamber and went in. A few minutes later, he returned, an astonished look on his face.

"Change of plans." Rogal looked around the bridge for anything that could be useful. "We need to buy some more time."

Brunner nodded and said, "Sir, I have an idea."

Rogal's eyes stopped roaming around the bridge and fixated on Brunner. This was going to be interesting.

Chapter Six

Everybody held their breath when the cutting torch stopped. A moment later, the bridge door was blown inward by a light blast. Then all hell broke loose. Every team member kept firing toward the blown entrance. Even Brunner. It was a good thing the corridor outside the bridge was narrow. Otherwise, the onslaught of OCU security forces would have been unmanageable.

The enemy forces took the worst of the blaster hits. The small FHM team were well protected where they were positioned. Brunner was able to monitor the progress of the upload from where he crouched, behind the conn. He still managed to squeeze in a few blaster bursts from time to time.

But it was too good to last. Hernandez got hit square in the chest and fell to the floor, writhing in pain.

"Cover me!" yelled Landon, as she left the safety of her position to drag Hernandez out of the line of fire.

With the extra man down, the enemy forces upped their attack with increased blaster fire. Rogal signaled Landon to take Hernandez into the core chamber. Then he pulled out a percussion grenade.

"Dalton, Brunner. On the count of three, get into the core chamber." Rogal readied himself to pull the grenade pin.

"But who's going to finish the upload?" Brunner protested.

"I can handle it. You get your ass into the core chamber when I get to THREE."

Rogal signaled the count with his fingers. ONE. TWO. He pulled the pin from the grenade and lobbed it toward the corridor outside the bridge entrance. THREE.

A loud boom sounded, and the sudden change in air pressure made Brunner's ears pop. The enemy fire halted briefly, allowing both Brunner and Dalton to run and take cover in the core chamber. From there, they positioned themselves while Rogal ran to the conn where Brunner had been situated a moment ago.

After the brief pause, the firefight resumed as if nothing had happened. Except now, the bridge entrance wasn't adequately covered. The OCU soldiers seized the opportunity, maneuvering onto the bridge and strategically placing themselves to cover every section of the interior.

From where he crouched, Rogal now had to cover multiple positions. The vantage point from the core chamber entrance was limited, so the task of keeping the OCU forces pinned down lay on Rogal's shoulders.

As the fighting continued, Brunner saw the display console on the bridge light up green, replacing the progress bar. Rogal saw it at the same time and repositioned himself to start the transfer protocol to the remote tablet.

Just before Rogal was able to punch in the last command of the protocol, a blaster shot hit him and knocked him down. Landon and Dalton let loose a barrage of fire at the position from where the shot originated. The OCU soldier was nearly incinerated by the onslaught.

"LT, can you get up?" yelled Dalton.

No response. But they could see that Rogal was still breathing. The remote tablet was still flashing a steady green and dangled by its attached wires beside the console.

"I'm going to activate the transfer protocol and retrieve that remote," said Brunner. "I need to go now. Cover me."

Brunner looked at both Landon and Dalton for the signal. The two grunts looked at each other and then nodded at Brunner. Then they turned and fired at the OCU soldiers on the bridge.

Brunner ran toward the console, grabbed the tablet, and activated the transfer protocol. While the transfer was underway, he raised Rogal to a sitting position.

Rogal opened his eyes and said, "What are you doing? Leave me and take the tablet with you. That's an order."

"I'm not leaving you, sir. Today is not your day to die. And if it is, I didn't get the memo."

The tablet beeped to signal completion of the transfer. Brunner grabbed it and disconnected the wires. Then he shoved the tablet into a sleeve of his uniform and took Rogal by the arm.

Landon and Dalton provided cover fire as Brunner stood and hoisted Rogal onto his shoulders. They raised their eyebrows in surprise by Brunner's sudden show of strength.

Brunner ran toward the core chamber entrance amidst the enemy fire. Just before he reached the entrance with his heavy load, Brunner took a blaster hit on his leg. He immediately collapsed, spilling Rogal onto the floor.

In quick succession, Dalton pulled Rogal into the chamber while Landon ran into harm's way to retrieve Brunner. Once everyone was safely in the core chamber, Dalton shut the chamber door.

Brunner didn't scream even though the searing pain in his leg made his eyes water. Fortunately, the protective clothing he wore had taken the brunt of the blaster hit.

"Help me up," he said to Landon. She grabbed his arm and yanked up hard.

Brunner stood up and hobbled toward the input terminal. From there, he activated the door lock. "We're safe for now."

Landon assessed the various injuries sustained by the team and administered the necessary first aid.

Rogal was fully conscious now and requested a status report.

"Sir, we have control of the ship," said Brunner, as he ran a quick diagnostic on the remote tablet to ensure its functionality.

"Great. Let's see what it can do." Rogal grimaced as he braced himself to stand.

A faint vibration surged through the small chamber followed by a low hum. The team stiffened up with alarm.

"Don't worry. I just fired up the engines. We'll need it for what's about to happen next," said Brunner, as Rogal sidled up beside him to watch the tablet screen.

Brunner activated the turret cannons and locked onto various targets in the OCU outpost.

"Watch this." Brunner switched on the display monitors in the core chamber and pressed the **<FIRE>** icon on the tablet screen.

Immediately, the turret cannons fired and destroyed the outpost's defense grid.

"Now we can take off without enemy fire." Brunner pressed another icon, and the vibration of the ship increased.

The team sensed the ship lift off. Everyone braced themselves as it continued to climb.

"What about the OCU security on board?" asked Dalton.

"I have a surprise for them," said Brunner. He called up the controls for the external docking ports and hatches.

Dalton watched the monitor as the ship's altitude increased above eight thousand meters.

Brunner hit the release button, and every docking port door and hatch opened up, dropping the inside pressure to zero in a matter of seconds and sucking out anything that wasn't attached to the structure of the ship. That included OCU soldiers. Anyone not sucked out would die of asphyxiation and boiling internal fluids, anyway.

"I don't understand," said Dalton, his eyebrows furrowed in confusion. "Why aren't we affected?"

"It's because this chamber is sealed from the rest of the ship with its own life support system," answered Brunner. "I suspected as much when I first opened the chamber door and heard the air hissing. I confirmed it when I checked the ship's schematics and discovered a secondary life support system. I put two and two together and made a wild guess."

"You made a guess with our lives?" asked Dalton, incredulously. "What if you were wrong?"

"But I wasn't," answered Brunner. "Besides, it was our last resort. I don't know what the big deal is. You were prepared to blow up this ship with us in it."

"But that's different. It—"

"Dalton, suck it up," said Rogal. "We've all taken worse chances. Sit down and enjoy the moment."

The rest of the team murmured in agreement.

Chapter Seven

"LT, why the change of plans? I thought we were blowing up the ship," asked Dalton.

"You can all thank Brunner that your pathetic asses aren't hamburger." Rogal held up the beetle-shaped metal object. "Understand that what I am about to tell you is highly classified. But you've put your lives on the line and deserve to know."

"What is it?" asked Landon.

"This is what is known as a Guardian Emulator. We don't have much information about it, but we do know it was invented by them." Rogal held up a flashlight and shone it in the direction of the fallen rafter beam that Brunner had bumped into earlier. Part of the beam rested on a crushed chair. It was hard to discern at first, but then the gasps from the team followed as they realized what it was. Sitting in the chair was the dead body of an alien. Part of its head was crushed by the metal beam.

"I think I fell on it earlier. What or who is that?" asked Brunner.

"That, my friends, is or was a Gardonian," answered Rogal.

"A what?" asked Landon.

"A Gardonian," he repeated. "The ka'Thar are known to have destroyed many races in their quest for universal dominance. Tragically, the Gardonians are among those races. The ka'Thar and OCU can never know we possess what may be the Gardonians' greatest weapon. It can change the outcome of the war."

The team fell silent as they reflected on the accomplishment they achieved for the Versapiens, for humanity. Even the ever-verbose Dalton was quiet.

"Brunner, is the ship back to normal pressure yet?" asked Rogal. This time his voice was gracious and low.

Brunner checked the instrument panel and nodded. He was back in his element now and confident in how to proceed. "Yes, it's ready." He unlocked the chamber door from the control console, his ears popping as the air hissed between the core chamber and bridge.

Landon helped Hernandez to his feet while Dalton assisted Farkas. Before they left the chamber, each one of Brunner's teammates gave him a light punch on his shoulder as they passed. Brunner smirked when Landon gave him a flirting wink and a thankful, yet joyful kiss.

It was the first time since Brunner had joined the resistance that he felt he belonged. He was part of the tribe now.

As he walked toward the chamber exit, Brunner felt a firm pat on his shoulder. Rogal was by his side, following closely.

"Well done," he said proudly. "Well done. Now take us home."

If you enjoyed this title, I would appreciate your leaving a review of the book. Good reviews encourage an author to write as well as help books to sell. Good reviews can be just a few short sentences describing what you liked about the book without having a spoiler. If you could spend 30 seconds writing a review, I would appreciate it: you can review this title right now at your favorite retailer.

Here is a preview of **another story** you may enjoy:

Tomorrow's Past: The Time Guardian Thriller Series - Book 1

Year 2428 at the Free Humanity Movement (FHM) Headquarters (50 Years Post-ka'Thar World Invasion)

THE EXPLOSION resonated throughout the cavernous chamber, raining chunks of the ceiling, some large enough to kill, on the fleeing staff below. Thankfully, most of the personnel were gone, having been forewarned only moments before.

Sonia was not so lucky. A chunk of rock, deflecting from the side of the chamber in an altered trajectory, struck her squarely on the head. She collapsed on the cavern floor, unnoticed, while others rushed around in panic mode.

Nobody thought to check on Sonia.

When she came to, she realized she'd only been out for a few minutes, judging by the continued commotion. The first thing she noticed was heavy dust in her mouth and nostrils from the broken concrete surrounding her, pieces of the once protective walls and ceiling changed now into weapons. Dry particles stung her eyes causing tears to flow, blurring her vision further. She wiped her face with a chalky-covered hand, making it worse. By the time her senses had returned, Carson, the unit supervisor, had spotted her and yelled for a medic. Both he and the medic made their way to her, dodging the debris on the littered floor.

She staggered to her feet and swayed for a moment before leaning against the wall for support. Glancing around, she saw others in rougher shape than she and waved the medic away. "Please, attend to her first." She pointed to Camille, one of the maintenance crew, who was bleeding from a head wound. While the medic went to check on Camille, Carson gave Sonia a quick once over before letting her go.

Sonia probed her head with tentative fingers, confirming a massive bump, and blinking against the pain. *I've had worse. I'll live.* She pushed off from the wall with shaking arms and stumbled a few steps. Pausing for a moment to regain her composure, she walked on unsure feet toward the briefing room and her father, Commander Garon Rogal. He'd be wondering where she was, worried about her condition.

"There you are," said Commander Rogal. He looked at Sonia then glanced quickly away. She could tell he was struggling to keep an unconcerned expression on his face. Her disheveled appearance and a scrape on her forehead didn't help matters but she knew he wouldn't comment. Sonia had a tough enough time proving herself to her peers without the top commander of the Free Humanity Movement (FHM) showing favoritism, even if it meant putting her in harm's way.

"Sorry for the delay," said Sonia. "Nothing I couldn't handle. They're getting close."

"There's a bigger issue at hand," said Rogal. "We're about to begin the briefing. Please take a seat."

Sonia grabbed one of the few empty seats near the front and gingerly eased her into it. On the screen behind Rogal, a recording of the security feed showed the attack from outside. A bright flash from the display caused Sonia to squint her eyes and then the feed went dead. Big red letters flashed across the screen.

Enemy attackers identified—OmniClon Universal Attack Forces.

Sonia found this amusing, despite the annoying ache in her head. Of course, this was the work of the OCU. *Who else would it be?*

If you enjoyed this sample then look for **Tomorrow's Past: The Time Guardian Thriller Series - Book 1**.

Here is a preview of **another story** you may enjoy:

Cyber Heist: The Cyber Heist Files - Book 1

GIORGIO KEPT his eye on the red LED numbers of the clock on the wall. It read 4:58 PM and seemed to have been stuck at that time for the past two minutes while he closed all the applications on his holo-screen. The droning sounds on the office floor had already died down as others closed their workstations and prepared to leave. He was getting impatient. Why are the last two minutes before the start of a long weekend always the longest?

The administrative offices of the World Government were going to be closed for three days. Giorgio had his entire weekend planned, but it depended on him making it on the next shuttle out. If he missed this one, then the fifteen-minute wait for the next shuttle would mean he would miss his 5:45 PM flight to Parisio. Because of the long weekend, the next available flight wouldn't arrive at the vacation city until well after midnight.

Sharla was already in Parisio, waiting in the luxury suite Giorgio had booked months before. He had planned a romantic evening, starting with dinner and then dancing. *Dessert* would surely follow later, something he was looking forward to more than an expensive dinner.

When the clock changed to 4:59 PM, he breathed a sigh of relief and pulled out his briefcase, ready to dash out of the office in less than a minute. His co-workers were already starting to move toward the exit doors.

That was when his computer uttered a small 'bleep' and his holo-screen lit up from sleep mode.

Giorgio stared at the flashing icon on the computer screen. "Dammit. Wonder what that's all about?" he said mainly to himself. There was a glitch in the waste management system. These server farms, can't live with them, can't trash them. When they were first implemented way back when, they worked beautifully. Very few problems and only a small number of hiccups here and there.

Over the years, as capacity was added to handle new divisions, increased traffic, and data processing, the piecemeal build in the system architecture resulted in the use of patches to mend the seams between various systems. But the damn patches weren't meant as a long-term solution. Each one weakened the whole system.

As per protocol, Giorgio called his supervisor, Clarence, who was not going to be happy after last month's cyber fiasco. He hoped Clarence was still in his office. Otherwise, he would have to call his supervisor on the emergency line.

From past experience, Giorgio knew Clarence would never answer his emergency personal communicator outside of work and preferred to respond to voicemail at his leisure. It could mean at least a half-hour delay before Clarence would return the call. Hating himself for not ignoring the glitch and dashing out the door, Giorgio held his breath as he listened for the line to connect on the other side. One, two, three rings.

If you enjoyed this sample then look for **Cyber Heist: The Cyber Heist Files - Book 1**.

Other Books by Freddie Kim

- The Time Guardian Thriller Series

- The Cyber Heist Files

Get the latest update on new releases from the author at:

https://www.freddiekim.com/newsletter/

About the Author - Freddie Kim

As a child, Freddie Kim would make blanket forts and refrigerator-box space ships, both essential things needed to repel against invasion from an alien race. Freddie has never really grown up from his childhood fantasies. The inspiration that he draws from the memories of his youth is captured and revealed to all in his writing.

Connect with Freddie Kim

I really appreciate you reading my book! Here are my social media coordinates:

Friend me on Facebook:
https://www.facebook.com/FreddieKimAuthor/

Follow me on Twitter:
https://twitter.com/freddiekimauth1

Check me out on Goodreads:
https://www.goodreads.com/author/show/16961603.Freddie_Kim

Subscribe to my newsletter:
https://www.freddiekim.com/newsletter/

Visit my website: https://www.freddiekim.com/

9 781773 500782